R.L. 3.0
PTS. 0.5
TST. 196440
LG

SIMPLY **SCIENCE**

The Simple Science of SOUND

by Emily James

CAPSTONE PRESS
a capstone imprint

A+ Books are published by Capstone Press,
1710 Roe Crest Drive, North Mankato, Minnesota 56003
www.mycapstone.com

Copyright © 2018 by Capstone Press, a Capstone imprint. All rights reserved. No part of this publication may be reproduced in whole or in part, or stored in a retrieval system, or transmitted in any form or by any means, electronic, mechanical, photocopying, recording, or otherwise, without written permission of the publisher.

Library of Congress Cataloging-in-Publication Data
Library of Congress Cataloging-in-Publication Data is available on the Library of Congress website.

ISBN: 978-1-5435-1226-7 (library hardover) — 978-1-5435-1228-1 (paperback) — 978-1-5435-1230-4 (ebook)

Summary: Learn all about sound and how it's made

Editorial Credits
Jaclyn Jaycox, editor; Brenton Slingsby and Ashlee Suker, designer; Tracy Cummins, media researcher; Kathy McColley, production specialist

Photo Credits
Getty Images: Steve West, 19; iStockphoto: Imgorthand, 6-7, 20-21, PeopleImages, 5, RBFried, 4, shironosov, 11; Shutterstock: Abd. Halim Hadi, 14-15, Alexander_P, 21 inset, Artram, 24 Design Element, Concept Photo, 11 Inset, Dragosh Co, 8-9, Dudarev Mikhail, 9, 29 Inset, Evgeny Karandaev, Cover, lewald, 25, 31 (giraffe), LuckyImages, 16-17, M-86, 26, MAHATHIR MOHD YASIN, 13, Martin M303, Cover Back, 2-3, 30 (speakers), 32, Mirexon, 12-13, NEstudio, 16 Inset, Paul_K, 28-29, SpeedKingz, 27, Tom Myers, 24, vkilikov, 10, wavebreakmedia, 22-23, Yuliya Evstratenko, 18

Note to Parents, Teachers, and Librarians

This Simply Science book uses full color photographs and a nonfiction format to introduce the concept of sound. *The Simple Science of Sound* is designed to be read aloud to a pre-reader or to be read independently by an early reader. Photographs help listeners and early readers understand the text and concepts discussed. The book encourages further learning by including the following sections: Table of Contents, Glossary, Read More, Internet Sites, Critical Thinking Questions, and Index. Early readers may need assistance using these features.

Printed and bound in the United States of America.
010852S18

Table of CONTENTS

How Are Sounds Made?...... 4
Sound Waves............... 8
What Makes an Echo?....... 12
Loud and Quiet Sounds..... 16
High and Low Sounds 22
Sounds All Around......... 26

Musical Glasses.............. 28
Glossary 30
Read More................... 31
Internet Sites............... 31
Critical Thinking Questions 32
Index 32

How Are Sounds Made?

A baseball smacks against a wooden bat. *Thwack!* Fallen leaves crunch under your shoes. *Crackle, crackle.*

Raindrops tap against your window. *Pitter patter, pitter patter.* We hear sounds all around us. But how is sound made?

Sound is made from vibrations. Tap a musical triangle. You can see it shake. As the triangle vibrates, it makes sound.

When an object vibrates, it bumps into the air around it. It makes the air vibrate too. When these vibrations travel through the air, they are called sound waves.

Sound Waves

Throw a pebble into a pond. Watch how the ripples move away from the splash. Sound moves in waves like the ripples in the pond.

Sound waves move in all directions from a baseball bat, raindrop, or anything else that makes sound. The waves travel through the air to your ears. But you can't see them. Sound waves are invisible.

Sound waves can travel through water.
Whales and dolphins hear sound waves in the ocean.

Sound can also travel through solids. Turn on a TV in one room. Then go into another room. Can you still hear the TV? The sound waves are traveling through the wall.

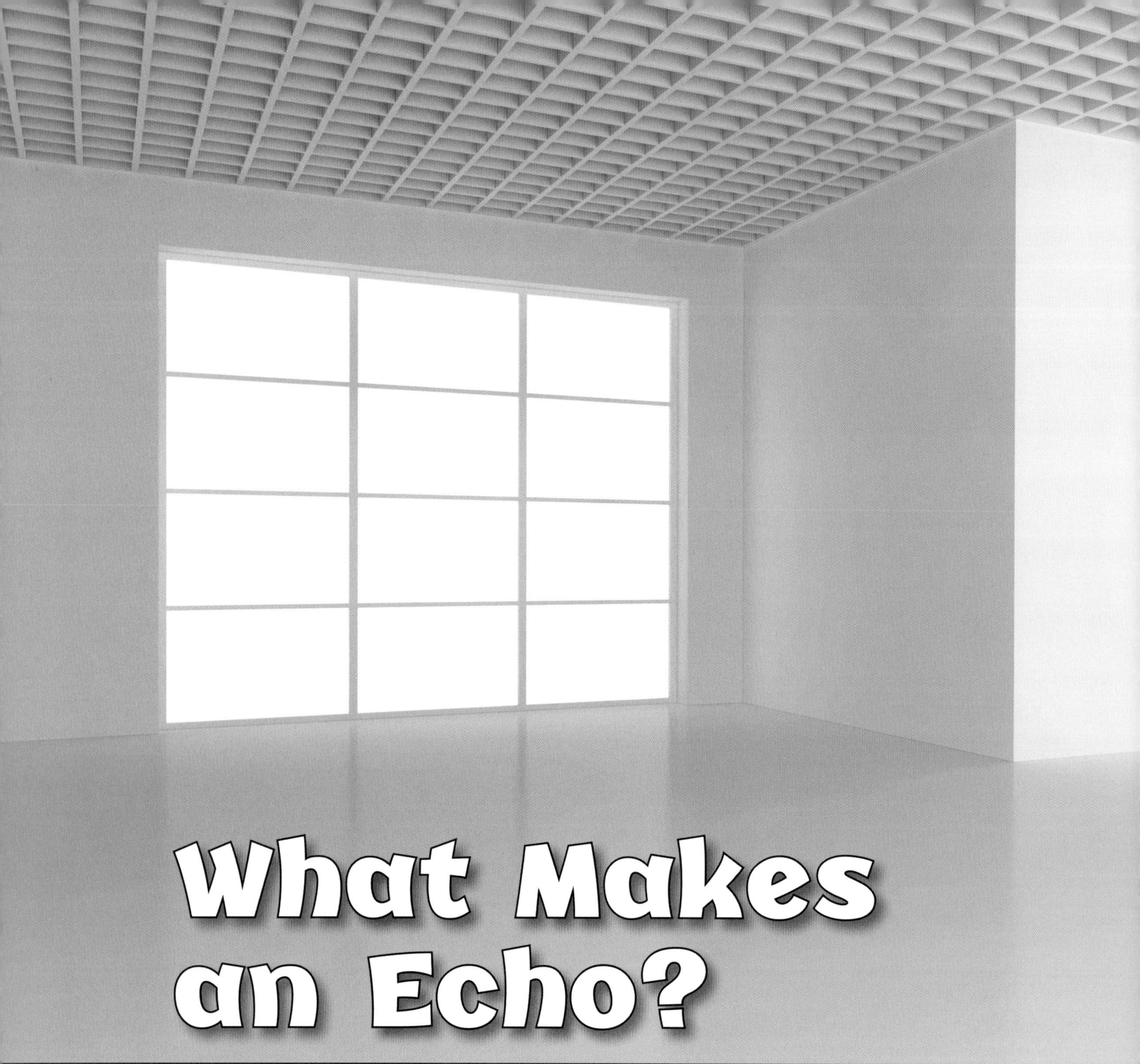

What Makes an Echo?

Stand inside a big, empty room. Now, shout your name. It sounds like someone is saying your name back to you.

Echoes are made when sound waves bounce off big, hard things like walls or mountains. They don't absorb the sound. Instead, the sound reflects off the object. When the sound bounces back to you, you hear it again.

Echoes can tell you how far away an object is. The longer it takes for the sound to come back, the farther away the object is.

Bats use echoes to find their way through dark caves.
As the bats fly around, they make squeaky sounds.
They listen for echoes to tell them where the cave walls are.

Loud and Quiet Sounds

Throw a rock as hard as you can into water. It makes big waves that travel far. Bang on a drum as hard as you can. The drum booms loudly. It makes big sound waves that travel far.

If you tap the drum lightly, it rumbles softly.
The sound waves are smaller and do not go as far.

Sometimes a sound is loud because you are close to it.
A whisper can be loud if your friend is standing next to you.

But a sound can be quiet if you are far away from it.
The roar of an airplane that is high in the sky sounds soft.

You can make a sound seem softer or louder. Put your hands over your ears. A sound seems quieter. You are blocking the sound waves. Take your hands away, and it seems louder. You are catching more sound waves with your ears.

When sound enters your ear, it travels through the ear canal to the eardrum. The waves move to the cochlea and then to a nerve. The nerve sends a message to your brain. Your brain figures out if the sound is loud or soft, high or low.

High and Low Sounds

Pluck the thinnest, tightest string on a guitar. You can see it vibrate very fast. Listen to the sound it makes. Things that vibrate quickly make high-pitched sounds.

The thickest string on a guitar vibrates more slowly. It makes a low-pitched sound.

Some sounds are too high for people to hear.
A dog can hear high noises that sound like silence to us.
This is called ultrasound.

Some sounds can also be too low for people to hear. This is called infrasound. Animals like elephants and giraffes use infrasound to communicate when they are far away from each other.

Sounds All Around

We hear all kinds of sounds around us every day. High sounds, low sounds, loud sounds, and soft sounds.

We hear horns honking, cats meowing, and people singing.
What kind of sounds can you make?

27

Musical Glasses

A sound can be high-pitched or low-pitched. It depends on how fast the object making the sound vibrates. Try out this experiment to hear the different sounds made by vibrations!

What You Need:
- 3 tall drinking glasses
- water
- spoon

What You Do:
- Line up your three drinking glasses. Fill up the first glass until it's almost full.
- Fill up the second glass so the water level is 1 inch (2.5 centimeters) lower than the water in the first glass.
- Fill up the third glass so that the water is 1 inch (2.5 cm) lower than in the second.
- Tap the top of each glass with a spoon.

Which glass makes the highest sound? Which one makes the lowest sound? Do glasses vibrate faster when they are empty or full?

GLOSSARY

absorb—take in and hold

cochlea—a spiral-shaped part of the ear that helps send sound messages to the brain

communicate—to share thoughts, feelings, or information

ear canal—a tube that helps sound travel from the outer ear the eardrum

eardrum—a thin layer of tissue between the outer and middle parts of the ear

echo—sounds that bounce off of things

infrasound—sound that is too low for humans to hear

invisible—something you cannot see

nerve—a thin fiber that carries messages between the brain and other parts of the body

reflect—to return sound from an object

ripple—a very small wave on the surface of a body of water

solid—a substance that holds its shape

sound wave—a wave or vibration that can be heard

ultrasound—sound that is too high for humans to hear

vibration—a fast movement back and forth

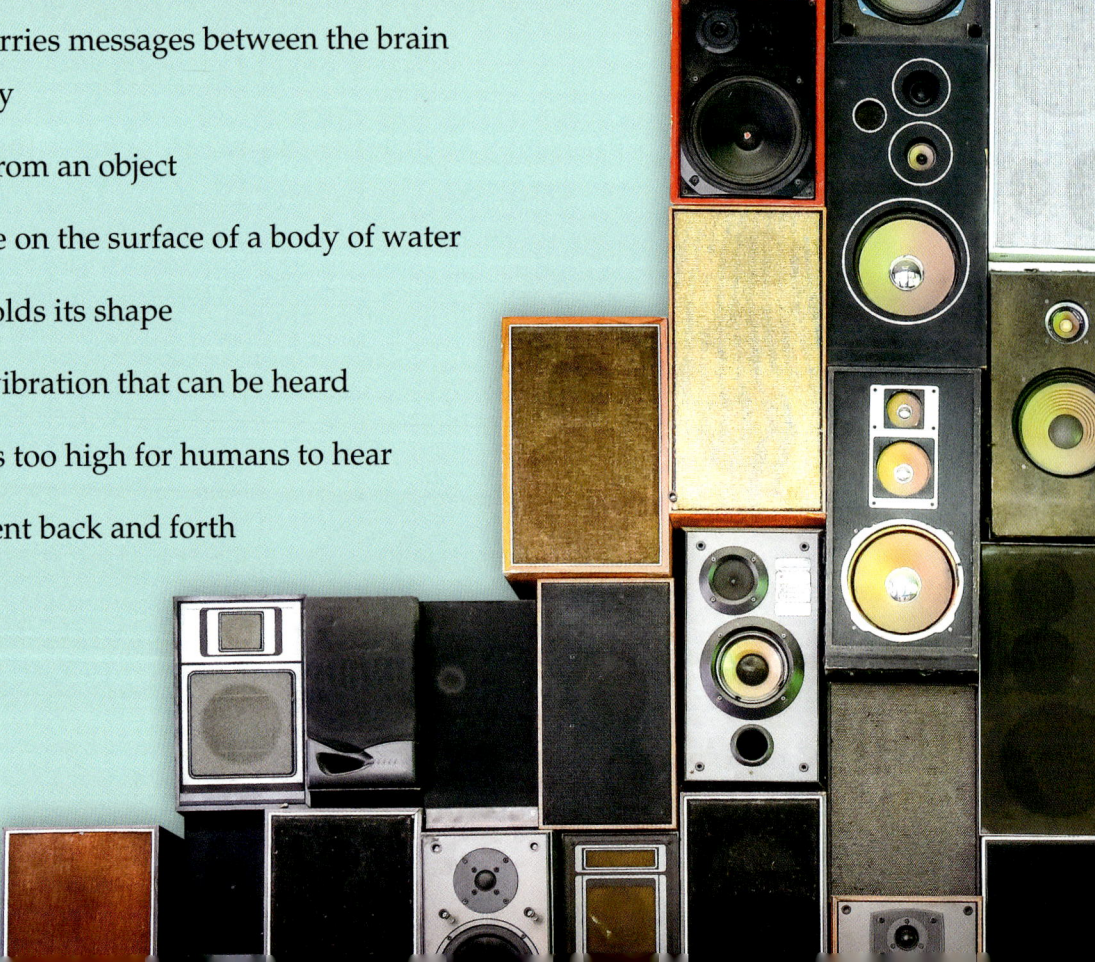

READ MORE

Boothroyd, Jennifer. *Vibrations Make Sound*. First Step Nonfiction: Light and Sound. Minneapolis: Lerner Publications Company, 2015.

Pfeffer, Wendy. *Sounds All Around*. Let's-Read-and-Find-Out Science. New York: HarperCollins Publishers, 2016.

Royston Angela. *All About Sound*. All About Science. Chicago: Heinemann Raintree, 2016.

INTERNET SITES

Use FactHound to find Internet sites related to this book.

Visit www.facthound.com

Just type in 9781543512267 and go.

Check out projects, games and lots more at www.capstonekids.com

CRITICAL THINKING QUESTIONS

1. Sound waves can travel through solids, like walls. Can you think of some other things sound waves can travel through?

2. When a sound echoes, it repeats. How is an echo made?

3. Some animals use infrasound to communicate with each other. What is infrasound? Hint: Use your glossary for help!

INDEX

air, 7, 9
animals, 10, 15, 24, 25
ears, 9, 20, 21
echoes, 13–15
infrasound, 25
loud sounds, 16, 18, 20, 21, 26
soft sounds, 17, 19, 20, 21, 26
solids, 11
sound waves, 7, 9, 11, 13, 16, 17, 20, 21

ultrasound, 24
vibrations, 6, 7, 22, 23
water, 8, 10, 16
whispers, 18